CYNTHIA C. DeFELICE

The Strange Night Writing of Jessamine Colter

Best wishes,

Cynthia DeFelice

Calligraphy by
Leah Palmer Preiss

Macmillan Publishing Company New York
Collier Macmillan Publishers London

Macmillan Publishing Company
866 Third Avenue, New York, NY 10022
Collier Macmillan Canada, Inc.
Printed in the United States of America

10 9 8 7 6 5 4 3 2

The text of this book is set in 13 point Goudy Old Style.

Library of Congress Cataloging-in-Publication Data
DeFelice, Cynthia C.
The strange night writing of Jessamine Colter.
Summary: Jessie, an elderly calligrapher who writes
announcements and notices of birth, marriage, and death
for the townsfolk, discovers that she has the ability
to predict the future in her writings.
[1. Extrasensory perception—Fiction.
2. Calligraphy—Fiction] I. Title.
PZ7.D3597St 1988   [Fic]   88–4325
ISBN 0–02–726451–3

Dedicated

to Buzz,
with love and thanks,

to Mary,
whose friendship I treasure,

and
to Phyllis,
who liked my story.

CHAPTER ONE

Jessamine Colter lived on the outskirts of town in a cozy little cottage that sat on the shore of a clear mountain lake. Once, in the year of the big flood, the cottage sat right *in* the lake. Jessie didn't mind a bit. She thought it was a great adventure to be living in the lake. She boarded up the front of the house, in case the waves hit it real hard, and spent the rest of the time fishing out the windows and paddling around the yard in the old rowboat. She was kind of sorry to see the water go back down, but the chickens were tired of having wet feet and no place to scratch for bugs.

Jessie's husband, Sam, had died many years before. The little house was all paid for, and Jessie made a bare living for herself selling eggs and doing calligraphy for the people in town. "Could you do this up in that fancy writin' of yours?" they'd ask, and they would bring her notices of births and deaths, posters for church suppers and county fairs, favorite sayings and quotes. At least once a year Mrs. Everhart hosted an elegant party and asked Jessie to write the invitations and place cards. And, each year, Jessie made up the school diplomas and wrote out a very special certificate announcing the winner of the Hoover Scholarship Award.

Once John Wilcox, blushing and lovesick, had brought her a poem to write up for him. It was a proposal of marriage, for he was too shy to ask his sweetheart himself. Jessie smiled whenever she remembered that. Betsy had said yes. Jessie had written out their marriage certificate and, in the years that followed, the birth certificates of their three children.

She smiled, too, when she thought about a day, almost sixteen years before, when she had filled out the birth certificate for a child named Calamine Williams. Callie was now Jessie's apprentice and a fine calligrapher in her own right, Jessie thought.

For almost fifty years Jessie had chronicled the life of the town. News of every event worth mentioning—and of some that weren't—had passed through her hand to the written page. Why, if you put all her writings together, it would be like a history book of the town.

Her most steady customer was Jacob Carpenter, who owned the restaurant in town. Jessie made up the menu for his restaurant in her fanciest style, embellishing it with swirls and flourishes, sprinkling in French words and using phrases like "stuffed with succulent broiled mushrooms" and "served on a bed of crisp garden greenery." Just reading it was enough to make your mouth water. Jake stopped by at least once a week to buy eggs for the restaurant and to bring her the newest menu items to write up.

"Hello, there, Jess. How's my favorite fancy writer today?"

"Just fine, Jake, except I've got a touch of arthritis in my hands again and it seems to be getting worse. Not a good thing for a calligrapher," Jessie answered.

"I've told you, Jessie, marry me and you'll never have to do another lick of work in your life. I'll spoil you rotten!"

Jessie laughed. "Now what earthly good would I be to you or anybody else if I never did another lick of work? Anyway, Jake Carpenter, that's what you say now, but before long I'd be doing all the cooking and cleaning up in that restaurant of yours, sure as anything. Besides, if I left here, who would feed my girls and gather their eggs?" And Jessie threw a handful of scratch to the hens gathered around her feet.

"Jessie, you're the stubbornest woman I ever met. One of these days I'm going to stop asking you, and then you'll be sorry!"

Jessie and Jake had this conversation every week. It had become a special joke between them, even though Jessie knew that for Jake it wasn't a joke at all. But, although Jake was her best friend in the world, she was happy just the way she was.

"What have you got for me this week?" she asked.

"Well, beef's gone up, so you'll have to change the price on that steak to $4.25. I'm adding mango sherbet to the desserts . . . pretty fancy, eh? And the special is going to be soup, salad, and chicken Parmesan for $3.50."

Jessie pretended to be shocked. "Jake, how many times do I have to tell you not to talk about things like chicken Parmesan in front of my girls? It makes them nervous and they don't lay right."

"Sorry, girls," Jake said. He chuckled, then added, "By the way, Jess, the Harvest Moon Dance is Friday night at the fire hall."

Jessie grinned. "I know, Jake. Who do you think made all those posters?"

Jake shook his head, saying, "I keep forgetting that you know about everything going on in this town before the rest of us do. But, in that case," he teased, "you've been just dying for me to get on over here and ask you to go with me, am I right?"

Jessie, her eyes twinkling, said solemnly, "I thought you'd never get around to it. If that's your invitation, I accept. And I'll have your menu changes ready. I'll do 'em up real special."

"You always do. I had some folks in from the city the other day saying what a fine-looking menu I've got." He paused. "Funny . . . they didn't have a good word to say about the food. . . ."

Jessie laughed. "See you Friday night."

CHAPTER TWO

Jessie finished feeding the chickens and went inside. She brewed herself a pot of tea, cleared off her desk, and got out her pen, nibs, and ink. She loved taking a clean piece of white paper and filling it with beautifully formed letters that were pleasing to the eye. Sometimes she marveled that only twenty-six letters could be put together in so many ways and for so many reasons, forming words that had the power to make a person laugh or cry, imagine a different world, think a new thought . . . or buy Jake's dinner special! Jessie laughed to herself as she finished writing.

Then Jessie cooked her supper, ate, and washed up. Now came her favorite time of the day. Taking a cup of tea and an old quilt to keep off the evening chill, she went out on the porch and curled up in the ancient porch swing. Sometimes she brought a lantern and a book, but tonight she just wanted to watch and listen.

She saw the moon rise and make a pathway of

light across the water. She listened to the geese honking out in the middle of the lake.

"Aaaah, Sam, the geese are back," she whispered. "It's a perfect fall night."

Whenever Jessie listened to the geese, she thought of her husband, Sam. Sam had been the best hunter, trapper, and fisherman in the county, and he had taught Jessie what he knew of nature's ways. She could still hear him telling her, in his slow, gentle voice, how the geese were able to make the long migration down from the Arctic tundra to the lake where they spent the winter, searching the nearby fields for food.

"They take turns being the leader, Jessie. Being the front goose in that vee formation is hard work. The leader's got to break the wind for all the others who follow. When the leader gets tired, he just drops back in the vee, and another, more rested goose takes over."

Sam's voice stayed so warm and strong in Jessie's heart that she felt he was still with her. In fact, she "talked things over" with Sam quite often. It wasn't that she fooled herself. She didn't pretend Sam was still alive or any such nonsense. No, it was more as if Sam had given her so much of himself

7

in their years together that he was simply part of her. She knew the things that would make him chuckle, and she could imagine his dry, witty comments. It helped her, at the end of the day, to sit and talk things over with Sam. Jessie knew most folks would call her crazy, but she didn't care.

All of a sudden, in the middle of her musings, she felt a strange urging. Without knowing why, she got up and went inside. She was drawn inexorably to her desk, to her pens and ink. She sat down. Her hand reached for the pen, dipped it carefully in the ink, blotted, and began to write:

Fresh Maine Lobster
with Lemon Butter
Tiny Broiled New Potatoes
Crisp Garden Salad
$6.50

Veal Scaloppine
$4.00

Persimmon Ice Cream
$1.00

Jessie looked down at the page. Bewildered, she read it aloud. "But what can it mean?" she wondered. "What is 'veal scaloppine,' anyway? And why did I write it?"

"Because you're getting senile, you old fool," she answered herself. She decided she must be tired and went to bed.

The next morning Jessie had all but forgotten the odd incident of the previous evening. She was up bright and early feeding the chickens, who were fighting over the corn as she scattered it about the yard.

"Now, girls, there's plenty for all of you, so stop the ruckus." Suddenly her face broke into a grin as she spotted Jake heading up the walk.

"'Lo, Jake," she called. "I didn't expect to see you again so soon. You're looking mighty chipper this morning."

Indeed, Jake was practically bouncing up the path, looking a bit, Jessie thought, like the cat who swallowed the canary.

"Jess, I'm so excited I feel like I'm going to bust! I just had to hurry over and tell you. I talked to a friend who owns a restaurant up in Maine and he's going to ship me forty fresh lobsters next week. And he gave me a recipe for something he calls veal scaloppine—says folks love it. And I'm adding persimmon ice cream to the dessert menu—what do you think of that? Jake's Place is going to be the most hifalutin'— What's the matter, Jess? You're looking as pale as whipping cream."

Jessie was standing, mouth agape, eyes wide. She collected herself. "I'm okay, Jake. I just felt a bit swimmy-headed there for a minute. I can't take all this excitement at my age, I guess." She gave a weak laugh. "Let's sit down and have a cup of tea, shall we?"

Sitting at the kitchen table, Jake talked excitedly about his plans. Jessie was tempted to go to her desk and show him the menu changes, already written, just as he had described them to her a few moments ago. How could she have known that this would happen? But it wasn't as if she had really *known* what she was writing last night. Writing those words had been quite beyond her will.

Deeply puzzled, Jessie decided not to say anything just yet about her strange night writing. It seemed too odd to talk about. Maybe it's just a coincidence, she thought.

But that night, as Jessie sat drowsily reading by the woodstove, she again felt an irresistible urging that drew her to her pens and ink. Her hand again reached for the pen, carefully dipped, blotted, and began to write:

*Laura Miles and Joe Walker
joyfully invite you
to attend their wedding
at 3:00 p.m.
on Saturday, December 12
at the Baptist Church*

"What on earth?" exclaimed Jessie, as she read what was written on the page. "Joe and Laura . . . well, of course. How nice. But how . . . ?"

Jessie pondered this. She had known Joe and Laura all their lives, had written their birth certificates and high school diplomas, had watched them grow up and fall in love. It was no great surprise, she reflected, that they would marry. Still . . . .

"Well, Jess, there's nothing to do but just wait and see. . . ."

CHAPTER THREE

The next day Jessie was on her way out to the henhouse with the old straw egg basket over her arm when she heard, "Jessie! Hi! It's me!"

"Why, Callie Williams, you're a sight for sore eyes!" She put down the egg basket and hugged the girl's thin shoulders.

"Oh, Jessie, I've missed you so much! It seemed like I'd never get over here with all my schoolwork and the chores. And Ma's been real bad. Oh, Jessie, I've got so much to tell you!" The words came tumbling out.

"Whoa, there, Cal!" Jessie laughed. "We can't catch up on two weeks' worth of news in two minutes. Let's have a cup of tea."

"I'll gather the eggs while you start the tea," offered Callie.

As Callie picked up the basket and ran to the henhouse, Jessie went inside. Putting on the kettle, she thought about what Callie had said. Jessie knew what it meant when Callie's mother got "real bad."

Alma Williams got "real bad" often, whenever she had money to spend on whiskey. Getting out the teacups, Jessie thought back to the day when she had first met Callie, six years before.

Jessie had been out repairing some broken fence in the chicken coop when she'd looked up to see a skinny girl about ten years old standing at the gate to the henhouse.

"Well, hello, child. Come on in, if you don't mind the smell of chickens. I'm used to it. What's your name?"

The girl looked stricken. Tears sprang to her eyes, and she stuttered, red-faced, "C-C-C-Calamine Williams, ma'am."

"Goodness, I must truly look a sight to make you cry just looking at me! Come on, let's go outside. I'll get the straw out of my hair and maybe I won't look so witchy."

Out on the grass Jessie picked straw from her hair and said, "There. Now, is that better?" She smiled at the girl.

"It's not you, ma'am. You look real nice. It's me. It's my—my name."

"What's the matter with your name? I remember

thinking, when I wrote up your birth certificate, that our names are alike. Jessamine and Calamine. I'm Jessamine, by the way, but most folks call me Jessie. What do folks call you?"

"Just Calamine—and I hate it!" the girl said fiercely. "The kids at school say, 'Calamine lotion, jump in the ocean!' My mother always says she wanted calamine lotion and, instead, she got me," the girl finished miserably.

Jessie had heard the story: Alma had had a bad case of poison ivy when Callie was born; two days later she was still itching and even the whiskey wasn't helping. "Calamine lotion—that's what I need," she'd muttered angrily to the infant lying in the makeshift crib. "I need *calamine*, not a skinny little brat whose father didn't even stick around to see her born." Suddenly, to Alma's drunken amusement, it seemed that she had found a fitting name for her child. "Calamine Williams," she had said, gloating. "That ought to make folks sit up and take notice!"

Jessie thought for a moment longer, then said, "Mmmm . . . it seems to me what you need is a nickname. I'm going to call you Callie. Would you like that?"

"Callie . . ." the girl said, listening to the sound of it. "Callie Williams . . . Callie . . . yes! It's perfect!"

"And maybe sometimes Cal for short, like people sometimes call me Jess, mmmm?" asked Jessie, lifting an eyebrow.

"Yes!"

"Okay, Callie Williams. Now let me tell you something. Don't you let folks make fun of your name. When someone asks, you speak right up and smile real big and say, 'Calamine—just like the lotion—but most folks call me Callie.' See, you say it before they do. Then there's nothing for them to poke fun at."

"Yes, ma'am. Thank you, ma'am," said the girl, her eyes shining.

"It's Jessie, not ma'am. From now on it's Jessie and Callie, you hear? Now, what did you come to see me about?"

"You're the lady who does that fancy writing, aren't you?" Callie asked.

"Yes, I am. That fancy writing is called calligraphy."

"Well, I think it's just so beautiful! I saw the place cards you made for Mrs. Everhart's party. I

1 5

was over there cleaning—I go there every week—and I saw them on the table. They look so elegant and nice! I saw my birth certificate once, and I thought even *my* name looks pretty, written like that."

"It certainly does, Callie."

"Well"—the girl took a deep breath—"I was wondering, if it wouldn't be too much trouble, could you teach me how to write like that? To do calligraphy? I—I don't have any money to pay you, but maybe I could help out with the chickens or—or whatever you like!"

Jessie looked serious. Then she said, "Callie, anyone who appreciates calligraphy as much as you do would be a joy to teach. You can be my apprentice. I know you have a lot to do already, but how about Sunday evenings? You could come for supper and then we'll work."

"I'll do all my chores early and be here Sunday night! Thank you, Jessie!"

That night, on the porch swing, Jessie had "talked over" Callie's visit with Sam. "Sam, that girl's something special. She's got an eye for beauty, although there's precious little of it in her life, poor thing. She'll be a hard worker, you wait and see. I need someone to pass my skill on to, Sam. You had to leave before we had a daughter of our own, and I think I could become real fond of that little girl. I just have a feeling. . . . Maybe Callie and I were brought together for a reason."

CHAPTER FOUR

Jessie's thoughts were jolted back to the present by the sight of Callie bursting through the door with the basket full of eggs. "I can't wait for the Harvest Moon Dance tomorrow night, Jessie! Guess what? A boy at school asked me if I was going. Do you think that means he'll dance with me? Well, anyway, if he doesn't, Jake will, won't he? You *are* going with Jake, aren't you, Jessie? He'll be heart-broken if you don't," she added, her eyes full of mischief.

"Yes, I am, and that's enough of that, young lady," said Jessie, pretending indignation. "Now, tell me, what's been going on in your life that's so important that you haven't been to see me in two whole weeks? I knew it had to be something big for you to miss your lesson last Sunday."

The animation left Callie's face all at once, and she looked deeply troubled. In a dull voice she answered, "It was Ma. She's been drinking worse than ever lately. Last Sunday night she went out and didn't come back and didn't come back, and I couldn't leave, not knowing if she was all right or not. She finally came home, but it was too late for me to come over."

Callie stopped suddenly, uncertain about whether to continue. It seemed strange, almost scary, to be talking about Alma. For as long as she could remember, she had kept Alma's secrets, telling people that, yes, everything was fine at home, even though it wasn't. She never talked to anyone about the bad times when Alma was drinking, not even to Jessie, though she often had the feeling that Jessie knew the way things were, anyway. Callie took a deep breath and decided to continue.

"Things have been pretty bad lately, Jessie. I don't mean to complain, but I just don't know what I should do for Ma. The worst part is that she promised me, after the last time, that she'd stop drinking. When she came home last Sunday night, I was trying to do my homework. I wasn't doing too well, I guess, because I was worried about her and wondering what had happened to make her so late. When she came in, I was so relieved. Then I saw that she was . . . well, drunk. I was so surprised because, you see, she had *promised* me. . . .

"I must have looked funny or something because she asked why was I looking at her that way—hadn't I ever seen a drunk before? Then she said, 'Who do you think you are? You're just the daughter of that no-good Alma Williams—and don't think you can change *that*. You're wasting your time doing all that schoolwork. They'll never give that scholarship to the daughter of a drunk!' "

Callie put her head down for a moment to collect herself. Then she looked up at Jessie with anguish, and the questions poured out. "Why did she say that, Jessie? And why did she break her promise? What can I do to make her stop drinking?"

Jessie led Callie over to a chair at the kitchen table, where they had spent so many happy hours working on their calligraphy lessons. She sat down beside Callie, keeping one of the girl's hands in her own. "Callie, do you remember when Jake decided he was going to retire from the restaurant business and just fish all day?"

Callie looked confused, then nodded.

"And do you remember how we told him that he would miss the restaurant, that he was too full of beans to retire? How we told him he'd be bored fishing every day? And he didn't listen to us, did he? He closed the restaurant and, sure enough, before a week was out he got bored and drove all of us and himself crazy, didn't he? Then *he* decided that retirement wasn't for him, after all, and Jake's Place opened up again. But there was nothing we could do to convince him until he was ready to believe it himself."

Callie said, frowning, "Yes, I remember, but—"

Jessie continued. "Well, Callie, honey, I think maybe that's the way it is with your mother. I know you want to help, you want to make things right for her. But sometimes there are things that people just have to do for themselves. You can't make her stop drinking, Cal. She has to do it herself. You might make her promise to stop, but if she's only saying it for you, she'll just break that promise and feel worse about herself when she does."

Callie thought for a while about what Jessie had said, then asked, "But why doesn't she want to stop, Jess? Why does she drink? I know it doesn't make her happy."

"I don't know, honey. Maybe something is hurting her real badly, and that's how she forgets. But until she decides that drinking hurts her worse, she'll keep doing it. And although it creates problems for you, Cal, it's not really your problem. You can't fix it, much as you want to."

Jessie was glad that Callie had brought up the subject of Alma. The girl needed someone to talk to. Jessie could see that at home Callie felt she had to be the one in charge, looking out for Alma, taking care of the chores, her job, and her schoolwork. It's almost, thought Jessie, as if Callie is the mother and Alma is her child.

There was another urgent question on Callie's mind. "Jessie, what about what Ma said about me? That I'm just wasting my time with school and all? She made it sound like someday I'll end up just like . . . well, just like her." The thought had been worrying Callie ever since Alma had said it. It frightened her.

"Cal, when people are drinking, they say things that hurt, things that don't make sense, things they don't mean. You listen to me carefully now, because this is important. Just like your ma has to be the one to decide how she wants her life to be, you are the only one who can decide what kind of person *you* want to be. And if you want to work hard and try for that scholarship, you go right ahead and do it. You don't have to be like your mother if you don't want to be. You're a separate, wonderful person named Calamine Williams, and thank goodness for that, because just think how lonely I'd be without you!"

Callie took a deep breath and said, "I'm going to have to think about what you said, Jessie." Smiling now, she added, "But I feel better already. What are we going to work on tonight?"

Callie's enthusiasm for their work sessions delighted Jessie. Just as she had thought, the girl was a quick learner and a hard worker. She knew all the different styles of script: Gothic, Italic, Bookhand, Celtic, Roman. She knew how to copy each style and how to choose which one would best enhance the text she was writing. She loved sitting at Jessie's kitchen table, everything cleared away except the crisp parchment and the pens and ink, the lantern shedding its soft golden glow over the pages.

At first Callie had been so discouraged! In her hand the pen had made no mark at all, then had suddenly let loose with a huge black blot. The paper had ripped as she pressed too hard. Her letters had been awkward, slanting in all directions, now too large, now too small.

"It looks so easy when *you* do it!" she'd cried.

Patiently, Jessie had taught her how to dip just the right amount of ink from the bottle, how to hold the pen with just the right pressure to allow the ink to flow smoothly, how to keep the pen at the correct angle to allow the letters to form properly. Now, six years had passed since those first lessons, and Callie's script was almost as beautiful and disciplined as Jessie's.

As they worked, Callie chatted about winning the Hoover Scholarship Award. "Just think, Jessie, I'll be able to go to art school. You always say I have a natural talent and a good eye."

"Wait a minute now, Cal. You know what we say in the chicken business: Don't count 'em till they're hatched. You can't be so sure you're going to win, can you?"

"Yes! I mean—I don't want to brag, Jess, but everybody at school says I'll win. I've got the best grades in the class!"

"Well, there's nobody's name I'd rather write on that certificate than yours, honey. I know how hard you work and I think you deserve it. But," she added mildly, "what if you don't win? Have you thought about that?"

Callie's face took on a stubborn look. "I've *got* to win, Jessie. I've got to prove to Ma that I can do it, that I'm not just wasting my time working and studying. Then maybe . . . well, maybe she won't think everything's so . . . so *hopeless.* Maybe she'll see that we *can* be different. Do you understand what I mean, Jessie?" she asked pleadingly.

Jessie sighed. "Yes, honey, I think I do."

CHAPTER FIVE

The following night brought the Harvest Moon Dance. The air was clear and crisp, the sky full of stars. The moon was rising huge and golden in the eastern sky, as if acknowledging that this evening was held in its honor. Jake and Jessie crunched through the fallen leaves as they walked up the path to the brightly lit fire hall. The fiddlers were tuning up as the hall, transformed by its decorations of cornstalks, scarecrows, and pumpkins, began to fill with eager townfolk.

Jessie waved to Callie and some of the other young people across the room. Suddenly the fiddlers struck up a lively tune and the dancing began. Jessie was happy to see Callie dancing with a young man, her head thrown back, cheeks aflame. Jessie twirled around so Jake could see Callie, too.

"It does my heart good to see that girl having such a fine time," said Jake. "And would you look at Joe Walker and his girl, Laura? I don't think they know the rest of us are here!"

The dancing kept up at a joyous pace until ten o'clock, time for the fiddlers to take a break and for the young folks to leave. Jake and Jessie said good-bye to Callie and walked over to the refreshment table. As they sipped their punch, they were approached by Laura Miles and Joe Walker, holding hands and beaming with happiness.

"Oh, Jessie," said Laura, "we've got the best news! We're getting married! Will you write out the invitations for us?"

A shiver ran down Jessie's spine. No coincidence, she thought, not this time. In her mind she saw the invitation already on her desk. She wondered giddily if Laura and Joe knew the date and time yet. She was struggling to think of the appropriate words to say when everyone began turning to the door, their faces registering surprise and dislike.

Alma Williams was standing there, swaying on the arm of a man Jessie didn't recognize. It was obvious that they had both been drinking. Jessie watched as Alma and her companion lurched onto the dance floor and the fiddlers began, obligingly, to play.

Listening to the half-whispered remarks and

watching the frowns on the faces of the other dancers, Jessie wondered, not for the first time, at the difference between mother and daughter. She thought of Callie's diligence at calligraphy, her hard work at school and at home, her open and friendly nature. Jessie was glad that Callie was not here to see her mother and to hear the whispered remarks.

The fiddlers seemed to sense the change in mood. They played a few more halfhearted tunes, then packed up to leave. The dance was over.

Jake and Jessie walked home in the bright moonlight, singing snatches of the fiddle tunes until they reached Jessie's door.

"Thank you, Jake. It was fun, wasn't it? Right up until the end, anyway. I think we outdanced just about everybody!"

"You know I enjoyed being there with you, Jess." He paused, seemed about to say something, then shook his head. "Now don't forget about those lobsters. I'm saving two for us."

"Well, I was hoping you were!" Jessie laughed. "Good night now, Jake."

"'Night, Jessie."

Jessie stepped inside, put a log in the stove, and settled down to talk things over with Sam.

"It happened again, Sam. I got chills all over when Laura and Joe told me their news. I'm afraid if I tell anyone what's happened, they'll think I'm just a crazy old lady. Or worse, they'll believe me, and folks will be coming around here to have me tell their fortunes or something ridiculous like that. Not that I could. I didn't know what I was going to write until I wrote it."

She paused, thinking. "If this is happening for a reason, I surely can't figure out what it is. Who knows? Maybe it will never happen again. . . ."

But two nights later, Jessie again got what she'd come to think of as "her feeling." She felt compelled to sit at her desk; her hand reached, dipped, wrote. She gasped as she read a notice of the death of Rufus McDonald. It was dated November 14, exactly two weeks away.

Jessie stared at what she had written for a long time. The fire died down to a few red embers. This news, revealed mysteriously by her hand, was different from Jake's menu changes, different from a wedding announcement. She did not know if the message was true. And she did not know what to do.

All night Jessie lay awake, thinking about Rufus McDonald. Rufus brought Jessie firewood in exchange for eggs. The firewood was worth a lot more than the few eggs Rufus took, but Jessie knew better than to offer him any money. Rufus was an old friend of Sam's, and Jessie knew he brought her the wood out of a feeling that went back a long way.

Lately, however, Jessie had been worried about Rufus. His wife had died a little over a year ago, and Rufus had seemed to go crazy with grief. For two days he'd kept Alice's body right in the house, refusing to admit she was dead. His daughter, Anne, had come to Jessie, begging tearfully for help.

"Mama's dead, Jessie, and Pa won't do any of the things that have to be done. He won't even listen when I talk of burying her. He won't say anything at all," she'd said, sobbing.

Jessie had gone with Anne, up to the McDonalds' cabin on the mountain, where they'd found Rufus sitting by Alice's bedside, silent and still as a stone. Jessie had sat with him all night, sometimes talking, sometimes quiet, never knowing if the unmoving figure by the bed was hearing her or not, for he'd never acknowledged her presence. In the morning Rufus had stood by, expressionless, as Jessie made arrangements for the burial. He had not attended the funeral, and in the months since, he'd remained distant and cold, even to Anne and Jessie.

Rufus had shown emotion only once. Three months after Alice's death, Anne and her sweetheart, Jim Walsh, had announced that they wished to marry.

"May we have your blessing, Pa?" Anne had asked.

Rufus had exploded with rage, saying, "So you want to desert me, too! Well, go ahead, but you won't get my blessing."

Jessie couldn't get used to this grim-faced, frightening stranger. She had tried to talk to him and break through to the gruff but kind man she used to know, but it had been no use. Now she knew she had to try again.

When morning came at last, Jessie got up, dressed warmly, put on her sturdy boots, fed the chickens, and started up the mountain. She found Rufus outside his cabin, chopping wood.

"Rufus, come inside and make us some tea. You and I need to talk."

Something in her voice or her face must have reached him, because he set down his ax and walked inside with her.

When they each held a steaming mug of tea, Jessie began. "Rufus, you lost your Alice and I lost my Sam. I don't know why it worked out that way, but it did, and we can't change that. But, you know, Sam has never really been lost to me. He's with me all the time. I talk things over with him. It helps me to think of what Sam would do or say in a situation, what Sam would think about something. I think Alice is still with you, Rufus, but you won't let her speak to you. I know you're angry with her for dying and leaving you, but *you don't have time for that.*"

Rufus looked at Jessie for the first time. She saw how pale and thin his face looked, but there was a glimmer of life in his eyes.

"This is going to sound strange, Rufus, but please listen to me. If I'm right—and I think I am—

you're dying. You have two weeks left. I say this because I seem to have a power that allows me to know about certain things before they happen. I've wondered why. It might be so that I can help you now."

Rufus stared at Jessie. She reached out and took his hand, held it as she said, "Rufus, please let Alice back into your heart. Listen to her. What would she say about the way you're living now? Is it what she would want for you? For Anne? For that beautiful grandson whom you don't even know? You have two weeks, Rufus. Two weeks to *live*. If you don't use them, you might as well die right now."

Rufus was silent for a long time. Then he reached for Jessie's other hand, and, after a while, his wide shoulders began to heave with sobs. When Rufus's body was still at last, he raised his head and looked at Jessie with the eyes of the man she used to know.

He said simply, "Thank you, Jess."

On November 14, Rufus McDonald died, chopping wood outside his mountain cabin.

After the funeral, his daughter said to Jessie,

"It's the strangest thing, but I don't feel sad that Pa is dead. He seemed to know it was coming somehow, and he talked about how happy he would be to be with Mama again. He came to see us, you know, every day for the two weeks before he died. You should have seen him with Peter! If he had lived, I'd have the most spoiled son in the world! I'm so thankful he came back into our lives."

CHAPTER SIX

All through the cold winter, the memory of Rufus's joyful final weeks warmed Jessie's heart, as the firewood he had left her warmed her cozy cottage. She snuggled next to the woodstove, sometimes reading and sometimes just listening to the fire crackling and the sounds of the night. But, at least once a week, she would find herself drawn to her desk; her hand would reach for the pen and write.

Many events in the life of the town were revealed by her hand that winter. Jake's menu changes were always written out before he came to tell her about them. Jessie smiled as she wrote the announcement of Betsy and John Wilcox's new baby girl and again, a few days later, when she heard that Betsy had given birth to little Sarah. She chuckled out loud at the invitations to Mrs. Everhart's New Year's Eve party, thinking how odd it was that she knew about the party before the hostess!

In time the gray days of winter gave way to the

first trembling signs of spring. Jessie sensed the restlessness of the geese out on the lake. Any day now, she knew, they would leave for the still-frozen north country where they would build their nests and raise their young. One morning she watched them lift off from the water with a great clamor and a purpose to their flight.

"Good-bye," she called. "I'll be watching for you in the fall."

Several weeks later, on a warm evening alive with the calls of the spring peepers, Callie and Jessie sat at Jessie's kitchen table, hand-lettering the diplomas for the students soon to graduate.

"Remember, Callie," said Jessie, "to us they all begin to seem the same, but a diploma is something that is saved forever, and it must be beautiful."

Callie came to her own name on the list and said, "Jessie, would you do mine? It will seem more special that way."

Jessie filled out Callie's diploma, noting proudly that Callie had earned highest honors.

When they had finished, Jessie walked Callie out to the yard, checking the gate to the henhouse as she always did. After saying good night to Callie,

Jessie stood for a moment, listening to the peepers'
song, then went inside.

It came upon her suddenly, as it always did, the
now-familiar feeling that led her to her desk and
pens. This time her hand reached for the heavy
parchment, the highest quality paper she used, the
paper reserved for documents of great importance.
She watched as her hand formed the distinguished
heading for the Hoover Scholarship Award. Then
it wrote the words:

In recognition of
sustained meritorious performance
in scholarship and leadership
the Hoover Scholarship Committee
is proud to present
The Hoover Scholarship Award
to
Kate Marchand

"Oh, no," said Jessie. But she looked at the
certificate and knew with certainty that it was true.

She thought of Alma at the Harvest Moon Dance, remembered the stares and whispers of the town-folk, some of whom were on the scholarship committee. They don't know Callie as I do, she thought. Perhaps Alma had been right; it would be easy for them to think of Alma and wonder what her daughter would do with a scholarship.

Jessie imagined Callie seated in the auditorium on graduation night, waiting breathlessly for the announcement of the winner; then Callie with her hopes dashed, crushed and humiliated in front of everyone.

"Poor Callie. I've got to tell her."

The next day was Saturday. Jessie went to Callie's house and was relieved when Callie said that her mother was not at home. "But what are you doing here, Jessie? I mean, I'm glad to see you, but—"

"Callie, I have something important to talk to you about. May we sit down?"

Callie, puzzled by Jessie's visit, pulled two chairs up to the kitchen table.

"Callie, I'm going to tell you something that you're going to find hard to believe. I hardly believe it myself sometimes. But listen and trust me.

"In the last few months I've been given a sort of gift—a power to know about certain things before they happen. It comes to me through my calligraphy. At night sometimes, when I'm alone and at peace, I get the strangest feeling. It leads me over to my desk, and I write. And what I write about later happens. I've known about lots of things: little things, like the circus coming to town, and big things, like Rufus dying."

Jessie stopped to see how Callie was taking this startling announcement. The girl was sitting as if entranced, her eyes wide, hands clasped tightly together.

"I don't always like what I learn," continued Jessie. "But nothing can change what's coming, and, well, it can help to be ready for things ahead of time. Callie, honey, Kate Marchand is going to win the Hoover Scholarship Award. I wrote out the certificate last night."

Callie's hands unclasped and gripped the edge of the table as she stood up. "Jessie, no! Why are you saying this? It can't be true—you know her grades aren't as good as mine! It's not fair! It's *not* true, is it?"

Callie's eyes suddenly widened and she said

wildly, "Throw it out! Throw it away and write it over again, Jessie, with *my* name on it. Please, Jessie, do it!"

Shaking her head sadly, Jessie said, "Callie, I can't do that. I don't make things happen. I just write about them before they do happen."

"Have you tried it? Have you tried writing something and seeing if it comes true?"

Jessie shook her head.

"Then how do you know you're not *making* things happen?"

"I just know, Callie. Making things happen isn't a power I have or would ever want to have."

"You can't be sure until you try it, Jessie! Just try it!" Callie's voice was rising desperately. "Just put my name on it!"

Jessie was quiet for a moment. "Callie, honey, please—"

"Oh, what's the use?" Callie wailed. "Ma was right. I was stupid even to try! No one cares what happens to me!" She turned and ran from the house, leaving the kitchen door swinging behind her.

Jessie sat for several moments in the Williamses' kitchen. Then she got up slowly and let herself out.

CHAPTER SEVEN

That evening Jessie was making her usual rounds of the chicken yard before closing it up for the night. She looked up to see Callie at the door to the henhouse.

"Evening, Callie. I was hoping you'd come," she said.

"Jessie, if you're finished, can we talk?"

"Of course. Why don't you go start some tea? I'll be right in."

When the tea was ready, they went out on the porch. Callie pulled up a chair across from the swing. She took a deep breath.

"Jessie, I'm so sorry for the way I acted today. I was wrong to ask you to write the award over again—wrong to run away like that. And especially wrong to say no one cares about me when"—Callie's voice was trembling and she struggled to control it—"when you've been so good to me. I guess I never even let myself think about not winning that award. I thought of it as my way out—my chance to have a life different from Ma's. And for a minute, after you said I wasn't going to win, all I could think was that Ma's right, and the whole idea of trying to make something beautiful out of my life is just crazy."

Callie stopped a moment and swallowed hard. "But I've done a lot of thinking today, Jessie. I'm not going to give up just because I didn't win the award. If I can't start school full-time on a scholarship, I can still go. I can work and save money to go part-time. Jake keeps saying the restaurant is getting too busy for him to run alone. I'm going to ask him if he has a job for me. And there are other ways to earn scholarships. Once I start school and they see what I can do, they might think I'm good! But right now I'm just going to find a way to *start*, even if it's only one class at a time."

Callie's voice had been getting louder and stronger as she spoke. She seemed to realize it suddenly, smiled sheepishly, and continued more softly. "Anyway, Jessie, that's what I've been thinking about today—that, and how stupid I acted. I know you told me only because you wanted to help me. It's just that it was all so *surprising*, finding out I wasn't going to win, and the strange way you knew it. It gave me the funniest feeling. . . . I—I don't know why I ran away like that."

Jessie smiled wryly. "Believe me, Callie, when all of this started happening, I felt mighty peculiar, too. You had a bad shock, honey, and you needed some time to work it out."

Then she held Callie by the shoulders and looked at her in the lantern light. "You know, Callie, I always longed for a daughter. And then you came along, a skinny little thing wanting to learn how to do 'fancy writing.' I remember the first time I saw you standing at the door to my henhouse. Your face looked then the way it did tonight—half-determined and half-scared to death! I said to Sam that night that you were special, and you've never done anything to make me change my mind."

"Then you forgive me?"

"There's nothing to forgive." Jessie smiled.

"Do you think I can do it, Jessie? Go to art school, I mean? If I work and take my time?"

"I know you can, Cal. And you know something? It makes me feel a lot easier in my mind to see you making some real plans for yourself. You and I count on each other and that's good, but someday . . . well, I won't be around forever, you know. Not," she added with a twinkle, "that I'm planning to go anywhere, mind you. But it's just plain good sense to think ahead."

Callie's eyes filled again with tears. "Jessie, don't talk like that! Why, if anything was to happen to you, I wouldn't care what I did."

Jessie's voice became stern. "Now, Callie, don't let me hear any more of that nonsense." Then, more softly, "If anything happened to me, I'd want you to keep right on, just as I did when Sam died."

Then Jessie grinned wickedly. "Now, about this plan of yours . . . ," she said. "Are you sure you want to work for that rascal, Jake Carpenter?"

CHAPTER EIGHT

On Friday night the senior class graduated with all the pomp and circumstance the school officials could muster. Jessie watched proudly as Callie shook Kate Marchand's hand, smiled, and said, "Congratulations, Kate."

Jake and Jessie had a party for Callie the next day, just the three of them and a picnic lunch, floating lazily around the lake in the rowboat. Jessie and Jake argued good-naturedly about pie recipes for the county fair. Callie talked excitedly about her new job as hostess at Jake's Place.

"I figure I'll make enough to pay for one class each semester," she announced, chin high and eyes sparkling. "And with what I make this summer, I can start in the fall!"

It was a busy summer, and the time passed quickly. Jessie continued to write announcements of events that then occurred: Lucas Wetherby's pig won first prize at the county fair (as usual); Jake won a blue ribbon for his cherry-rhubarb pie (much to Jessie's chagrin); the fire house held an auction to raise money for a new hook and ladder.

Writing about things before they happened began to lose its strangeness for Jessie. The yearly pattern of events had a regularity and a symmetry that were, to her, beautiful. Posters for county fairs inevitably followed school diplomas, wedding announcements followed dances, births followed marriages, death followed life. Even Jake's menu changes reflected the endless cycles of the seasons: strawberries, new peas, and lamb in springtime; fresh vegetables and trout in summer; apple desserts, pumpkin pie, and turkey in autumn; roast goose and chestnuts in winter. When she finished one of her messages late at night, she would think, Yes, of course. The rhythms of the town's life were a part of her after all these years. She knew each person, had observed them and written about them all her life. Yes, she would think, of course.

All of a sudden, it seemed, the days grew shorter and the nights colder, the leaves colored and fell, and the geese returned. Settled in the porch swing, wrapped cozily in her quilt, Jessie held her cup of tea in both hands. The warmth felt good on her arthritic fingers. As she felt the chill in the air, she wondered how she'd be able to manage the woodstove during the coming winter. She listened to the familiar honking of the geese, the lapping of the waves, and she watched as each wave carried its small share of moonlight to the shore. The wind blew the dry leaves around on the porch, and her chickens made a few last clucks before settling themselves for the night.

Suddenly Jessie got her "feeling." She went inside and sat at her desk, and her crooked, aching fingers reached for the pen. Her calligraphy was as beautiful as ever, she thought proudly, if she wrote very slowly and very carefully. The hand finished its message. Jessie read it.

"So," said Jessie. "Well." She paused. "I'd better get things ready."

She wrote for a while longer, then arranged all the papers on her desk. She threw some extra scratch for the chickens and settled herself back on the porch swing with her quilt. Her mind wandered lazily back through the years of her long life. She thought about her childhood . . . her life with Sam . . . her friendship with Jake . . . her love for Callie

4 7

. . . her little cottage . . . her chickens . . . and the joy she had found in them all. Somewhere in the middle of her memories, she fell asleep.

The next morning Jake stopped by as usual. He checked the henhouse and, not finding Jessie there, he hollered through the back door. When he got no answer, he walked around to the porch.

"Jessie, where are you hiding?"

Then he saw the figure in the swing. "Come on, up and at 'em, Jessie. It's an apple-pickin' day."

As soon as he climbed the steps, he knew. Jessie sat curled up in the swing, wrapped snugly in her quilt, with a peaceful smile on her face. She was dead.

Jake picked her up, carried her inside to the bed, and covered her gently with the quilt. Some papers on the desk caught his eye. Brushing tears from his eyes, he walked over and read the beautifully hand-lettered notice of the death of Jessamine Colter. Next to it were the menu changes he had come to tell her about that morning.

EPILOGUE

Callie Williams sat on the porch of Jessie's cottage, swinging gently and looking out at the lake. It was her cottage now; Jessie had left it to her in the will she'd written on the last night of her life. Callie came here whenever she wanted to be with Jessie, for Jessie was everywhere here. Her favorite quotes still hung on the wall, her pens and ink sat on the desk, her quilts and teacups all remained in their places. The chickens squabbled in the backyard. Callie didn't mind if they listened while she talked things over with Jessie.

"I miss you so much sometimes, Jessie, I think I can't stand it. Then I think of what you said to me . . . about what you would want me to do if anything happened to you. I'm trying, Jessie, but I'm lonely without you. I think I understand now why you always used to talk to Sam. You were right—it helps. It helps to come here, too. I'm staying with Ma for now, but—you know something?—this feels like my real home. It always has."

She thought for a while, then went on. "Art school is really exciting, Jessie. I'm learning a lot. They told me they'd never seen calligraphy as beautiful as mine. I told them I had a wonderful teacher. A few people in town have brought me things to write up for them—Jake's menu changes, of course, and some other things, too. I try to do as good a job as you would."

The swing creaked as Callie rocked back and forth. "I keep thinking about how you knew about Rufus and the scholarship and even about the night you died. I don't understand it, Jessie, but I know this: You taught me that life is beautiful and mysterious and full of possibilities. I just wanted to say thank you, Jessie."

On the other side of town Jake, too, was talking things over with Jessie.

"I always knew you were something special, Jess, but I'm darned if I know how you knew about those menu changes." He paused, shook his head, and continued. "I just took the latest ones over to Callie. Thank goodness you taught her the way you did, or I'd have to start doin' fancy writin' myself!

"That girl's going to be just fine, Jessie, you wait and see. She's got a lot of you in her . . . stubborn, don't ya know." He chuckled. "Won't let go of the chickens—talked *me* into feeding them the mornings she's at school! She's a big help at the restaurant, too. Folks seem to like her. Yep, she'll be just fine."

He was silent for a while. "You know, this town isn't the same without you, Jess. . . . Still, for me, you'll always be here somehow. But I expect you know that, don't you?"